# THE WITCH VS THE STATE OF ARIZONA

FARON LEVRETS

*The Witch VS State of Arizona*

Copyright © 2024 by Faron Levrets.

**MILTON & HUGO L.L.C.**
4407 Park Ave., Suite 5
Union City, NJ 07087, USA

**Website:** *www. miltonandhugo.com*
**Hotline:** *1- 888-778-0033*
**Email:** *info@miltonandhugo.com*

Ordering Information:
Quantity sales. Special discounts are available on quantity purchases by corporations, associations, and others. For details, contact the publisher at the address above.

Library of Congress Control Number:      2024918262
ISBN-13:          979-8-89285-264-7      [Paperback Edition]
                  979-8-89285-263-0      [Digital Edition]

Rev. date: 08/19/2024

# The Witch
# VS
# The State of
# Arizona

The setting of this story takes place in a city. A modern world where there are normal people living in the city, but among the humans you have interesting creatures and the justice for the people are the lawyers who live among the people but possess a greater power as part Elvin. They fight crime but in a different way. For some strange reason the trend in the city has been catching witches, and the nasty hateful ones have been sentenced so far. You can read about it in the papers.

As a normal life takes place among the people, a particular lawyer sits at his desk checking on witches and what they have been accused of. He is also curious to know what magic these witches are using; who are their victims as he runs through his computer. Just then, he gets a particular call from a person who doesn't want to give any personal information other than finding out about a witch called the

Watchout. Now the lawyer goes by James as he's not familiar with this type of witch. The lady calling gives an address and people are missing.

He tells her I'll look into it and hangs up the phone. Now the lawyers in the building are very classy and dress nicely in suits but underneath that is a whole lot of mystery. They certainly work well together as a central justice system taking on crime and different cases in the world they live in, and they drive really nice cars.

Now as James starts his research looking for a Watchout, he is looking through the Book of Witches and all it says is spell cast needs more information. There isn't enough information for James to know about this witch. They take on all kinds of interesting cases. A goblin from the underground city to a troll underneath the bridge eating people. All kinds of weird things the lawyers are dealing with. Its dirty work but they are the ones to get the job done and it's not always pretty, not what they have to go through. You try taking on a blood lust vampire, it's not that simple. James begins his investigation among the other lawyers in the building. Finding out if they have any information on the Watchout, as he speaks to a few of his loyal co-workers who have been there for years. Oadee another Elvin is working on a witch hunt, James asking if he knows anything about a Watchout.

"Not really," Oadee replies, "She typically casts spells."

Then he asks Brian – one who is working on a case that mysteriously showed up about a Headless Horseman. Brian says I can't chat right now I'm on to something big right at the moment but I hear that witch is very dangerous be careful James.

James with no real leads decided to check out the anonymous person who called about the Watchout. It's getting late as he grabs his paperwork and his keys. He leaves the building and gets in his car. Just as he starts the car he sighs "It's going to be a long night."

He drives off to the address that was given about 30 to 40 minutes from here. Around these houses were businesses like restaurants and bars and he also notices a telephone booth if someone needed to use it for emergency or they simply weren't carrying a phone. He gets out of the car and knocks on the door. No one is answering the door, it's late at night, could be the reason not too many people open their doors to strangers during the night. James gets a little frustrated and begins to whistle out a beautiful melody, his eyes light up green as he sees what had occurred here during the time he got the call.

James has mysterious powers as he looks into the past. There is a lady calling someone at the phone booth as it starts to rain she hangs up and starts to run as if she saw someone chasing her. James looks down the street and sees a beautiful woman, he looks back the other way. She can hear the lady who is crying, "Just leave me alone."

James' eyes appear normal again as he just uncovered a scene getting prints from the toll booth; wondering who was that woman who looked very beautiful walking towards the lady that was running for her life. James gets back in his car and calls it a night heading home. As he gets to his place taking the elevator to the 9th floor and unlocks the door, he begins to unwind. After a hot shower, he does one thing he loves to do as well as most half breeds that are Elvin.

He opens up the pantry and it's filled with boxes of cereal. Like 10 to 20 different kinds with a great big bowl and lots of milk in the fridge. He pours out Rice Crispy cereal with a banana and some sugar – a perfect way to end the night while watching some NFL Jets vs Bills and a movie appears to be on Harry Potter Goblet of Fire. Then he's off to bed, now it's normal for Elvin people to have dreams as James falls into a deep sleep.

The Elvin breeds normally encounter dreams when they sleep, they find more information through these dreams to help solve their investigation, or they receive sometimes tangible evidence to help with the courts process. As James dreams, he is back where he was at the toll booth. He looks down the street where the lady starts to run for her life. James begins to chase after her, he says "lady, stop right there! Why are you running?"

As he chases her around the building. She quickly stops. With a panic she tells James, "I don't have much time but take this."

She says she can't be trusted. She is crying and runs again just as James was looking at this curious thing she gave him. He turns his head and sees an evil woman with a scary look. Just as she was about to cast a spell, it wakes up James from his sleep. James realizes its now morning a little after 8:00AM.

He sees in his hand a necklace with a ruby red gem. He looks into the red gem and sees something inside it – a human, as if it looks lost inside. He notices that she's trying to find her way out. The necklace must mean something to someone, why did she give it to me? James doesn't understand the necklace but keeps it with him. He grabs a bowl of Fruit Loops before he goes to work. Now James realizes he has a court proceeding at 12 in the afternoon. He is there to prosecute a witch –a case that he needed to convince the jury that's what she is: a bad witch.

Judge Metal Rocks walks in to begin the court hearing. Now James had tried to convince the jury from her appearance. Just by looking at her you would think that yeah, she looks like a witch. Her pointy nose, her eyes were popping out her face; looked pretty crazy, her hair was frizzy and black. Put a witch hat on and you would believe she's a witch. She fit the description but in this world, you had to prove she could spell cast. So, James had a plan it was more to entice the witch as he brought in a big cauldron to set up the questions to ask the witch. Now magic was allowed in court hearings as long as you addressed it to the judge and what it does.

The witch was caught by security as she shape shifted to hide her identity to get into a rock concert without paying her ticket. It says right at the gate, No Magic or You Love Witch Prison. As hundreds of fans came to see Pantera / Metallica.

"So, you walked in as a food vendor employee then you turned into a rock n roll junkie. Police arrested you when you were head banging as you were turning shapes is what they had seen, is that correct, Elvira?"

The witch makes no remarks. So, I bring to you today jury what that spell looks like. As you can see the cauldron is coming to a boil. The witch starts to twitch a little. You need two rattle snake tails, purple, red and green Skittles, a hog's nose, bad breath from a professor, as James keeps adding in more pieces to the cauldron the witch is getting more and more restless. Then dragon claws, last but not least music notes from Korn. The final ingredient, white trash from a bus stop.

James starts to mix the ingredients staring hard at the witch. This was the spell you used, wasn't it? As colors we're coming out from the cauldron. She said it is, she just can't resist any longer. You IDIOT! Say the magic words. She starts to sing a song from Korn

"Make Me Bad" (The song starts to play in the background) she's chanting spell words from the witches book very catchy indeed while she's head banging. She turns into a witch. Now you're thinking is this what a witch looks like?

She looks very attractive as she head bangs to her spell. Judge Metal Rocks finds the witch guilty for spell casting, fined and sentenced. The people in court were caught off by the witch's appearance. Court dismissed. James and his team are happy with the results and gets a win. But back at his office, James is wondering who is the lady being chased down the street. He's not sure who the lady is. He's going through the data files of the prints off of the toll booth. He's wanting to catch the Watchout eventually but first James wants to get an identification of the victim.

From the UK, a red head goes by the name Doll. The alias she goes by is Crystal or Palace; arrested for using coke and bath salts. Not a typical drug I would use, James is thinking out loud. Why is the witch chasing her? What is the reason. He looks again at the necklace. It is very mysterious with the lady inside. A lost soul, but beautiful necklace admiring the gem. He has an address where Doll lives. He's about to do more investigation on her asking about the necklace.

He finishes his day at the office, James drives over to the lady's house. He has questions concerning her and the necklace, it's getting late into the night as he arrives not too far from the toll booth. Several blocks away, he heads up the stairs to these apartments as he knocks, the door was left open. James calls out, "anyone home?" He walks in. James is curious if something happened as the door was left open. He walks in. There is no one in the living room; he checks the other bedrooms. James says, "Hello! anyone here? I have your necklace..."

As he walks in one of the bedrooms, he sees a woman dead in the corner of the room. Her body looked like someone had sucked the life out of her. James was wanting to know what had occurred or what troubled her. It was the woman who gave him the necklace. James again uses his mysterious powers – a soft whistle, as his eyes light up green. He uncovers the mystery as she walks in her house scared of something and she's crying. The lady in tears, I don't know what to do.... she hears a sound in the house, her heart is beating rapidly.

"Hello my pretty! Why are you running? With a cackle. I want only one thing." Doll is scared, she says out loud, why did I ask for my soul? Being scared the witch comes into the room. I want your soul you promised to give. She starts to spell cast on her taking her soul from her body. Then the witch in the room says STOP FOLLOWING ME! Give me my soul.

James' eyes come back to normal. The witch killed her. James walks out of the room, walking back down the stairs James walks out onto the street he looks down the road and sees someone but can't see their face. He hears her voice, "You are the one, a protector a guardian. I ask the voice nearby a question. Why did you take that lady's soul? Why did you kill her? There is a price to pay. What do you seek here?" He says I seek justice you're now a criminal to the organization of witch trials I need to bring you in dead or alive...

James boldly stands his ground through the voice. You have to catch me first. She laughs – a witch's cackle again, as the voice leaves.

She's still standing there I still can't see her as I begin walking towards her. I am moving towards her down the street, she starts to turn and walks away from me. I walk a little faster and she's walking a little faster. I decided I need to catch her before she causes any more trouble I slowly start jogging then a faster pace. She's now running as a witch hunt begins. She's running. I'm several feet behind, I can hear her breathing and the sound of her shoes when she runs. I'm following her as we enter the big city. In and out of buildings leaving the back door, I had just realized I better protect myself. I quickly look at my palm, I start drawing lines and quickly I whisper, protect me, as the lines start to glow a dark green color.

I'm not as vulnerable to magic as I'm still running knowing she's going to start casting some wicked spells. Now before things start becoming unpredictable or unusual I had not mentioned the witches book of spells. Now witches are all different. It's the type of witch you encounter. There's the demonic witch now she's just evil all around, she would send everyone to hell if it was her way of doing things. You have a witch who loves the cauldron this type of witch makes enchantments, shift shapes, lots of interesting spells. She might even try falling in love with you with a love spell. You have witches that try to eat children. Watch out for them it just makes them feel younger. They use aging spells for that very reason, some witches just want to have fun. Have you seen the movie Brave?

We'll be careful with witches. If you try asking for a witch to help you with your problems they just become bigger problems. Witches love spells and are not afraid to try anything. I believe that a witch comes with some sort of curse. They keep casting spells and more spells then it becomes trial and error, and a witches spell tends to backfire, meaning it just didn't turn out the way they expected it to go and it might eventually turn on themselves. Last but not least, the last advice I want to share with you. If you're offered an apple, you might want to ask if she's a witch, you take one bite and you might be sleeping longer than you think.

Now in the world of witches you do run into good witches there's not a lot of them left, but there are good witches that find ways to make life better for people.

Now if you fall in love with a witch, you better know what you're getting yourself into because that frog spell is just under her sleeve if you dare cross her witches' hat, don't piss her off. So where was I, oh yeah, I'm chasing this witch and she does one spell that really causes some confusion. She takes a seed and with a splash of water she throws it to the ground she says, "lost into the corn fields." Oh no she sprang a corn maze and I'm not sure who's in 't but it's not good people. My profession isn't as easy as you think it is but it's what we as lawyers live for. We catch witches for a living to make it a safe world for people to live in. That's our number 1-800-The Witch Trials. We take the calls and we win in court. But first, I'm having to do the hard part catching her. Right now, I'm kind of lost and what I encounter is a scare crow coming to life. I engage in combat rushing at the scare crow, I burst out a ball of fire and it begins to burn I conjure the wind and push it into the corn maze as it begins to burn.

As I push through the maze, I run into three more just like it carrying a sword. But I push out more fire to burn down the maze. I walk out of it safely as the witch escapes through her black hole. I walk through it back into the city where we just were. She escapes. I mark the dark hole with an Elvin mark as it turns green so it can't be used. I go back to my car and go home for the night, I say to myself I can't figure out what kind of witch I'm dealing with just yet. As I'm looking for a specification or class of witch. Hmmm, thinking as I drive home with that thought in mind, winding back down again with a bowl of Lucky Charms, it's time I turn in for the night. Before bed I grab a big green apple I say the words "Watch What I Eat" the apple turns red to green, I take a bite and put the apple on the night stand.

I don't want to consume any evil spell the Witches tries to make me eat. I begin to fall asleep. In my dream, I'm back at the corn field, I start to learn something about the witch as she casts a spell to make the black hole where we got out. She grabs a paint brush and makes a black line she say the words "Paint It Black" as she steps in and back into our reality.

I walk again through the black hole and I find myself in the darkness. I find myself being confronted by the witch asking questions, who are you? I stay calm. I'm James. Why did you kill a human? The necklace I have starts to light up again. She's asking, what are you? Are you human? I don't answer the Witches questions. I did say I'm human. She says, why are you following me? I told her I'm going to bring you in under the law of witchcraft, you killed a human; you took her life. She's angry and in her scary voice, this is none of your business human.

She yells out "STOP FOLLOWING ME!"

Her presence is close to me as she walks out of the darkness revealing herself, she gets close to my face. A scary witch she is, I say in a calm manner. I can't I will find you and have you sentenced to prison. She's laughing as she walks back in the darkness. I've warned you human take my advice and stop this or it will be your death at my hand. The darkness fades away. I see her fly off on a broom stick with a black cat. My dream ends. I sleep through the night and my alarm wakes me up. I grab another bowl of Cookie Crisp cereal and off to work I go. I decided to visit a unique antique store called Only Special Treatment. A friend I know works there, they have lots of weird stuff. I need to find out more about the necklace why is it glowing.

He's a warlock and gamer. I know that because he's always streaming Elder Scrolls; he loves that game. I walk in, looking at all the antiques, I see my friend with a greeting, what's up Brogee? that's his name. "Long time no see my good friend." So, he tells me how his game stream is going and asks, so what brings you down this side of town? I showed him the necklace I've carried around with me.

He's like, wow bro! you know what that is? He asks. I said "no" that's why I come to you; you're the genius.

That's a soul where did you find it?

I told him what happened previous during my dream. So, she gave you this?

Yeah.

That locket you carry is a lost soul. You know witches make those for certain reasons if someone is needing something in their life. You're holding onto someone's soul do you know that?

James responds why would someone keep their soul in this?

I don't know but that witch does. She must have asked the witch for something for her soul is my guess.

I say to Brogee, "thanks, I needed to know what this was."

He gives me more information, that witch is dangerous James, she's the only one that can release that soul back to her. But I don't know what she wanted you need to find out why she gave up her soul. That witch is a soulless witch they are uncommon they steal souls in exchange for who knows what.

I give my friend some money that's for information. He said thanks. He tells me one more thing: she casts undead spells James. Be careful friend. Driving to the office thinking about what is that an undead spell what does that do. I have a court proceeding at 1PM. I have to address to Judge Metal Rocks my case for Doll and I'm having to research this witch, if there is more information on her. We have plenty of resources as I am working through my day. I try to find what is a soulless witch and what we know about her. I open up the books of witches. I see it now under soulless witch. A witch without a soul. I see a description of Spell casting: Conjuring; can manipulate; very uncommon witch; she thrives off of dead people; witchcraft closest related to demonic witches; not too proud to beg. Deceitful. Don't ask her for anything. She likes games, playful, spontaneous; found only in certain cemeteries. Almost extinct.

I talk among the Elvin lawyers who work in our division, if they had a case with one. They all said no, I also go through certain channels if I can pursue this case against the evil witch, The soulless. It's likely to take on this witch but survival rate is 10%, good luck dude! As I'm reading through the witches spell book. Good luck! What does it mean by that? I'm scratching my head.

In ten minutes, I start my proceedings with the Judge. Now our Elvin lawyers are lucky to have Judge Metal Rocks.

Other judges aren't easy to work with on cases we handle among the human population. I take my place in the courtroom. Court is now in session all rise for Judge Metal Rocks. The judge is looking over the papers for the proceedings. Judge announces the case for Doll with an alias Crystal or Palace. Judge Metal Rocks goes over her records, served time for illegal use of drugs, charges on assault, dealing, prostitution. Judge asks James is there additional information on your investigation for Doll, James hands over her records from her medical history, she comes from an orphanage; she has been in and out of foster homes. She has records of being abused your honor. She has a history of PTSD/anxiety/schizophrenia. She was murdered by a witch your honor.

The judge is asking for proof of the murder or anything from the morgue. Yes, your honor, we have pictures. The judge looks carefully at the body. James gives details of her death, she looks brain dead but look at her eyes; her face looks badly deteriorated from the witch's spell. Any further evidence. James shows the judge the locket. Inside that locket your honor, there is a soul. She looks completely lost and that is Doll. Though her body lays waste, I can bring her back to life your honor.

The judge sits and thinks over this as he holds the locket with a beautiful red gem. Judge tells James normally in those cases we need to see a spell cast for evidence if she is still alive. But I can work with this if I have the information regarding your investigation for one who committed the crime. Who is the suspect? James brings out the book of witches on page 72 (Song by Tinashe-Vulnerable plays quietly in the background). I give you the soulless witch. I have encountered several times in my dreams. What is her spell cast? What is her ranking among witches? I don't have any cases on this witch, James, She can conjure. Her rankings are the deadliest of witches giving her a 10. Judge asks James, "why don't I have any information regarding a soulless witch after all these years James?" I'm just now learning about it. James says "there are few left in existence." Judge pauses for a little bit.

Judge Metal Rocks gives his final statement. "OK, James, because of the circumstances this is Oct. 9, 2023 I'll give you till Halloween then I'm closing the case on Doll, bring in this soulless witch and see if there are redemption and justice for Doll, I'm also granting you one special ability by your Elvin High Council. Do you need protection?"

I said, "Yes."

"OK your ability is granted. This case will proceed by the end of the month. Wish you the best and be safe out there James. I know we live in the darkest of times."

I'm back at my office and we have a lawyers meeting once a month going over the cases and criminals, we have each tried or cases still in existence. I explain my cases and tell the lawyers I don't have any more court hearings till the end of the month. I mentioned as well, I'm granted one special ability from the high council as I'm now hunting a dangerous witch. The other Elvin Lawyers speak out about an ability that might help during my adventure or witch hunt. They said the best spell to use for safety is a deflection spell called black light if she springs out a deadly spell upon you. The Elvin's tell me to be cautious and be dangerous James. We salute each other with the Elvin sign. Meeting dismissed.

I drive home that night I know I have to see the High Elvin District. It's not here among the human population it's in another realm. We only go there for special occasions. Meeting a more powerful division than the world we are from. I grab a bowl of Captain Crunch and I sleep well into the night. I get dressed the next day into a more mythic attire. As I call out the words of Elvin pulling me out of this world though the gate. I leave earth. Our world is a scenery of beautiful nature – an outside realm of waterfalls and mountains and green grass with lots of tall trees, entering into the land of our people. I meet the guard. "I'm here to see the High Council." He lets me through.

The Elvin people are highly thought of a stronger and mysterious people. I enter the council room, the judge sits high above as I look up at the council.

"We were expecting you, James" says the High Elvin Creed. We greet with the Elvin mark; I raise my arm.

"I'm here today asking for an ability against an evil demonic witch called the soulless witch, granted by the earth court, so I have come in that regard."

Elvin Creed says, "Your ability is granted. What do you seek?"

"Black light, a deflection spell for protection."

"Your ability is granted. Speak the High Elvin Words to be given this ability in the chamber of power. We also wish to upgrade your powers because we hear good things about you on earth. Speak the words of the gift of legends in the chamber of power."

The ground shakes below me as I'm being sent upward, I reach a point high above there is another door of entry, I walk in and I reach the chamber of powers. I see our Elvin language written and beautiful carvings of Elvin in the chamber. I say the words to grant me my gift of black light, lightning strikes as it turns dark inside. I can feel the rush of this new power given to me through my body. I then call out my gift given from the High Elvin council; A gift of legends mark. Speaking in Elvin language a powerful burst of light carries me off the ground for several minutes. I'm being elevated and feel the gift I'm getting as that burst of light burns through my body. I feel regenerated. More powerful than before. I leave the chamber of power speaking again in Elvin of gratitude. I return back to the high council room. I give my gratitude to the High Council in Elvin language for the gift of legends. I'm making my way to the portal back onto planet earth.

I feel different, maybe more powerful than what I was before. The mark of the gift of legends is engraved on my wrists. I wait till night falls before I start my witch hunt. I believe it's the fall festival. I get in my car. I turn on the radio listening to Korn "Got the Life".

I make my way to the Autumn Festival. The night is cold as I'm walking through the festival keeping a sharp eye out for the witch. I see some people I've never seen before, a girl holding a teddy bear with a back pack. I see a man flipping cards in his hand wearing a mysterious hat, with a tooth pick in his mouth. I see a red-headed women with tattoos. They kind of stood out. I see a tent that reads Free Tarot Readings. I walk in, I have a seat. I see before my eyes the witch.

My locket starts to glow. She holds a crystal ball, "Let's look at the past."

I pause in the moment she starts to cackle. I can hear the witch's voice as it shows a moment in Doll's life, she's taking drugs and abusing herself she walks in to meet the soulless witch, "I want a better life," as she's crying in desperation from trauma. The witch says I will give you that but you must give up your soul. She says ok. I tell her to wear this locket as I cast the undead spell on her. She doesn't feel the pain or trauma. I erased her memory. She's living a new life, I give her under my spell. But that would only last so long as her spell wears off and the witch comes for her soul. "You see human? Why do you care about her?"

I told the soulless witch to undo her spell and release her soul from the locket. "Human, what did I say would happen if you tried to follow me?"

I begin to speak the Elvin language trying to break the witches magic hitting her with a breaking spell. She stops for a few seconds, she was stunned, being thrown off guard, and she gives me a nasty grin "trying to take away my magic." She casts a spell. "Let's have some fun," as the festival becomes a circus changing the theme.

Her magic is unstable from my spell, I started to walk around this circus of clowns, I see up ahead a beautiful woman, I believe it to be the witch I'm looking for. She smiles at me as she enters a mirror maze. I decided to walk in. I knew I was walking into something dangerous. I go inside, it's not what I was expecting to see. I'm seeing the witch in twenty different mirrors. I knew the witch is deceiving.

I call out another Elvin spell "you must be me" as three clones walk outside of my body. She begins to question me. My clones are distracting the witch as mirrors begin to break. She's trying to seduce me with her beauty in the mirror. She's asking my deepest desires, she's asking if I find her attractive. I begin to question the witch, "The night she came to you she wanted something from you. Doll was disturbed, she wanted a better life, you manipulated her didn't you, witch?"

She's still talking in her sexy voice. I mentioned, "you used her, didn't you? Your spell only lasted so long, giving her temporary moments of happiness but you knew in a few days it would be gone." More mirrors begin to break. She turns back into that evil witch and leaves the maze of mirrors. My clones come back to me entering my body. I continue to follow the evil witch. We venture through the circus. She begins to drop fire in three different places. From out of the ground comes a knight of death.

I use my Elvin powers and I arm myself with steel on a white horse with a two-sided bladed axe. We charge at each other, with a swing of my axe, we collide blade to axe, we charge again, blade to axe. A third time as he drops his sword he uses dark magic, carrying a ball of fire in his hand. I lay down my axe and use an Elvin spell 'The Arrow of Light'. We both charge each other I quickly throw the arrow of light, barely dodging the ball of fire. I knock him off his horse. I move quickly getting off my horse, I grab the axe and swing at the undead knight removing his head from his body. I'm really starting to hate this witch even more.

The trouble she's causing, the annoying illusions – I'm starting to lose my patience, aggressively hunting her down. I throw another breaking spell trying to stop her from using magic. Again, she creates another illusion, we are in a hospital setting. The witch calls out to me, "human, why do you care so much about her?"

As I look she's overdosed on drugs and the doctor is trying to bring her back to life, she flat lines and came back. The witch makes a point. I tell the witch boldly, "It's her fate to die that way, but you killed her! You created a spell; you took her life. It ends here witch. Give her back her soul!"

I call out in the old Elvin language. "Learn of the undead."

I bring up her past. The witches life was taken by another witch. It depicts the witch becoming cursed. You gave up your soul to be cursed by another witch. James learns of her story; her fate. The witch begins to sob. You can see her tears drop on her face. She starts a loud moaning of sadness. James says, "I can see your pain."

She faces me in combat. Finally, the last phase, as she draws a sword, I begin to use my powerful spell, "Black Light!"

Right when she swings the sword, I break all her magic. I keep my hand at her when releasing the spell granted to me by the high council. It's draining her seeing her body lose energy. I tell her to re ease her. She says okay; she finally submits. I stop casting black light. She falls to the ground unconscious. I move close to her body and write the Elvin words on her hand, stopping her from using witch craft. I bring her into a prison to be sentenced for spell casting on Doll and the witch trials she caused in Arizona for the murder of nine other souls.

Court is now in session. All rise for Judge Metal Rocks. The victim whose soul is taken lays in a glass covered casket brought in by James' team of lawyers. The Soulless Witch enters in with shackles on her legs and hands with a ball and chain. She looks weakened as she slowly walks in her spells and magic have been taken away by James.

The day of Halloween. James tells the judge, "This is the witch that has taken Doll's soul. She spell casted to take her soul your honor. I'm here today to prove she's an evil witch."

The judge says, "please present the evidence in the case of Doll vs The Witch."

I take the locket – this beautiful necklace, and put it on Doll's neck. I tell the witch to release her soul. The witch in sadness has her head down, she looks at me for a moment then she looks at the judge. She begins to say the words, "this soul that's lost is now I find. I bring back this life I took that I claimed was mine. I release you from this curse of mine. This soulless witch claims souls to bind. The joy you had and the things you see were temporal in your reality, but now you live in life I give your free from darkness and all that's dead."

She then sucks in air and breathes out cold air that floats to her locket releasing her soul. Doll is gasping for air. She wakes from an empty corpse to a living person. She sits-up from the glass covered coffin. The audience in court was shocked. The judge begins the sentence of the soulless witch and the nine deaths that were taken in Arizona from her evil spells. The last end of the story gives a historical account of a real-life witch trial that occurred in Arizona.

The End

www.ingramcontent.com/pod-product-compliance
Lightning Source LLC
Chambersburg PA
CBHW020342130626
46549CB00003B/1250